Text by Mark Kimball Moulton
Illustrations by Stewart Sherwood
© Copyright 2001
All Rights Reserved. Printed in the U.S.A.

Published by Lang Books
A Division of R. A. Lang Card Company, Ltd.
514 Wells Street • Delafield, WI 53018
262.646.2211 • www.lang.com

10 9 8 7 6 5 4 3 2 1
ISBN: 07412-0867-9

The Traveler's Gift

Written by Mark Kimball Moulton • Illustrated by Stewart Sherwood

For Megan and Liam,
and for my godchild, Victoria.

Stewart

This book is dedicated to Barbara in Montana,
Monica, Yvonne, Ronnie and all my old college buddies,
with a special dedication to Michael,
my magical traveling companion, and his family...
and that little rascal Queenie, of course!

Mark

Presented to _____

on this Date _____

from _____

AS A CHILD,
I truly did believe in
OLD SAINT NICK
up North...

who flew through winter's moonlit skies each December twenty-fourth.

AND ON CHRISTMAS DAY,
the twenty-fifth,
I'd wake and rush to see
what treasures
wrapped in pretty bows,
he'd left beneath our tree.

And, like all good, happy children,
I'd cry with joyful glee
at each and every gift I'd find
left 'specially for me!

But it was not 'til I was older,
perhaps aged nine or ten,
that I received the special gift
I've treasured most since then.

Now, this really may surprise you
that the gift of which I speak
was not a doll nor ball nor bear
nor clothes from a boutique—

It was offered by a wanderer,
a traveler of the land—
I only chanced to meet him once...
never since, you understand.

But I'm getting much more before myself—
the proverbial "cart before the horse"—
so I'll start at the beginning
and recount all in its due course...

Christmas Day had come and gone—
New Year's Eve had long since passed.
The earth was slowly shrugging off
the winter's long, cold blast.

The day was warm and quiet
with a lovely, little breeze—
but I was feeling sad and blue
and slightly ill at ease.

I was sitting in a hollow
throwing pebbles in a pond,
watching as the ripples there
stretched on...
     and on...
         and on...

I recall that I was thinking
just how sad life had become—
so many things were going wrong
and nothing seemed like fun.

I wasn't doing well in school,
my best friend had moved away...
and, worst of all, we'd just found out
Grandma had taken ill that day.

I wished that I was all grown up,
my troubles far behind.
I would have given anything
to find some peace of mind.

I saw my own reflection
in the water, crystal clear,
then watched while my reflection blurred
as my eyes filled up with tears...

I rubbed my eyes and, as I did,
I saw my image change.
It no longer looked at all like me,
but like someone very strange–

Where the water once reflected
my own young and tear-stained face,
now an old and wrinkled one
was mirrored in my place!

I turned and, much to my surprise,
  behind me stood a man–
with plump, red cheeks and snow-white hair,
and a long staff in his hand.

He wore a torn and tattered coat
with patches here and there–
and, o'er his back, he held a sack
with bulges everywhere!

As strange as all of this may seem,
I didn't feel scared.
Something in his soft, brown eyes
told me how much he cared.

He never asked what was the matter,
never queried why I cried–
just dropped his bag and, with a groan,
he sat down by my side.

"You know," he said, "sometimes it feels
that everything's gone wrong–
but sure as seasons change, you'll find,
this, too, will change 'fore long."

With that, he reached inside his sack
and rummaged for awhile,
then handed me a clear, glass globe
and told me with a smile...

"Hold this globe and shake it, please,
and tell me what you see—
for these old, weary eyes of mine
sometimes play tricks on me."

So I took the globe and shook it
and inside, what did appear—
but Santa in his bright, red sleigh
pulled by his flying deer!

Now this was nice, but nothing new—
I'd seen such globes with snow—
But what happened next astounded me...
for that ball began to glow!

Then, tiny stars appeared inside
that twinkled bright as day!
Santa smiled, he waved at me...
then faded right away...

The sphere began to glow again
and the snow inside grew thick.
I was amused, but thought that
this was just some kind of trick—

But, as I watched in wonder,
that deep snow began to drift–
and there I was on Christmas Day
admiring a gift!

"Why, I remember this!" I cried.
"It was only just last year
when Mom and Dad gave him to me!
   I love that wooly bear!

"But I'm confused...how can this be?
Something must be amiss!
How can I see myself in there?
What kind of *globe* is this?"

   "Why, a very special, magic globe,"
   he told me with a wink,
   "and if you'll sit and watch awhile,
   you'll learn a lot, I think!"

With that, the scene began to change,
and replace the one before—
    and there was Grandma blowing kisses
    from her own front door!

She looked so calm and happy—
quite contented, it was plain—
so peaceful that I soon found I
was feeling much the same.

The snow began to swirl again,
though I didn't move at all—
and a different scene began to form
inside that crystal ball.

Once more I saw myself in there,
though now I seemed *years* older—
and I looked like my own father
   with a baby on my shoulder!

Something seemed familiar
in that baby's tender face—
something 'bout the way she looked
that I could not quite place—

and then she turned and gazed at me
and to my great surprise—

> I *saw my own dear Grandma*
> *in that newborn baby's eyes!*

I thought I saw a little bit
of Mom and Dad there, too—
perhaps the color of her eyes,
that startling, dark blue.

A single tear slid down my cheek
and dropped upon the sphere...
and I began to understand
the sequence of things here...

The snow inside the magic globe
blew 'round and 'round again,
and when it settled down this time,
my child was nine or ten.

Again, it looked like Christmas day
with presents 'round the tree.
My child was holding up a doll—
she laughed and ran to me—

She kissed me and she hugged me—
my eyes filled with loving tears...
and then I understood just what
Mom and Dad had said for years...

"It's YOUR joy that makes us happy—
when you're older, you'll believe—
It *really is much better, son,*
to give than to receive."

One final time the snow began
its magical ballet–
and once again, St. Nick appeared
in his tiny, bright red sleigh...

His reindeer bucked and snorted
and the sleigh began to rise–
then Santa called these words to me,
which I found very wise...

Treasure your most precious gift – don't wish your time away!

Let Christmas reign throughout the year – Celebrate your life each day!

HO★HO★HOOO!

The traveler winked and smiled at me—
then ruffled up my hair.
He nodded once and slowly
   he just vanished in thin air!

His image glimmered once before me,
like a misty, soft moonbeam…
then *poof!*…he was gone in the next second,
   just as silent as a dream.

He'd left without a whisper—
disappeared without a word.
I shook my head, confused and dazed
by all I'd seen and heard.

   "Where have you gone?" I wondered—
   "or…were you ever *really* here?
   Did I just *imagine* all I saw
   inside that sphere?"

But I knew that what I *felt* inside
was *very real* to me—
and I was thankful to that man
for all he'd helped me see.

I must have spoken this out loud,
though now I cannot say—
    "Please, sir, will you come again
    and visit me one day?"

And from far off in the distance,
'cross the pond and through the trees,
I heard these words float back to me
upon the warm spring breeze...

"It's time that I should journey,
slowly wind my way back North,
but, count on this—
I'll *visit each December twenty-fourth!*

'Til then, my friend, remember—
    Life's a gift from up above.
Appreciate each moment,
and cherish everyone you love!"

That was the last I heard from him—
never saw that man again.
But I could feel his spirit with me,
every now and then...

Especially at Christmastime,
I felt him *all* around—
in every act of love and joy,
his spirit could be found!

I've listened to his sound advice—and held it close each day—
it's made my life more meaningful in every single way.

For the wisdom that he offered me was honest and sincere...

★ ...that

LIFE IS TO BE TREASURED

every day of every year! ★

★

The End

Other Books to Collect by
Storyteller Mark Kimball Moulton

• • •

Caleb's Lighthouse

A Snowman Named Just Bob

Everyday Angels

The Night at Humpback Bridge

Reindeer Moon

One Enchanted Evening

Miss Fiona's Stupendous Pumpkin Pies

A Cricket's Carol

The Visit

Teddy's Friendship Quilt